Desiree Mull

DUNCAN
THE DELIGHTFUL DASCHUND

A New Home

Copyright © 2007 Desiree Muller

REFERENCES:

1. Animal Talk Magazine. South African Publication

2. Staffordshire Bull Terriers by Anna Katherine Nicholas. T.F.H. Publications, Inc

3. Southern African Birds. A Photographic Guide by Ian Sinclair. Struik Publishers

Chapter 1

Dunky

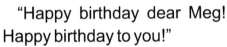

"Happy birthday to you! Happy birthday to you!"

A small arm appeared, pushing the duvet off the tussled, chestnut hair. One eyelid wearily stretched open, while the other remained squashed into the pillow.

"Happy birthday dear Meg! Happy birthday to you!"

Meg focused her open eye on the two blurred figures in front of her. Her Mom and Dad! It was Saturday, wasn't it? Why

3

weren't they allowing her to sleep late? What was Mom proudly holding up - forcing Meg to open her other eye?

A puppy!

Meg bounced upright, causing her a second's blurred vision as the blood rushed from her head. She felt a tiny, smooth, living thing, moving on her lap.

As her eyes focused in front of her, she saw a tiny, ever-so-cute Miniature Daschund on her soft duvet.

"You bought him for me!" she shrieked as she picked up the startled little puppy and pressed his tiny body into her neck. She gave the little animal a gentle hug.

"Well, you did earn him, dear. You deserve him for being such a good girl this year," beamed Dad.

"Yes, although he's your birthday gift, each time you see him, know that because you've worked so hard at school you've earned him," smiled Mom. Indeed Meg *had* earned the little puppy. Each test that she'd performed well in at school had earned her a part of the puppy's tiny body.

"His name is Duncan," Mom gave the puppy a pat.

The puppy squirmed in Meg's hand. "He's ever so cute! But Duncan is such a grown up name, I'm calling him Dunky." Meg jumped up and down on her bed and the puppy bobbed up and down on the cozy duvet.

"We should introduce him to the rest of the family," beckoned Dad. Mom followed him.

Meg, gently clutching the puppy, padded barefoot down the passage and outside onto the patio. She felt scared. How were the other pets going to react to the new family member?

Chapter 2

Coco

Dad guided Coco, the Staffordshire Bull Terrier, closer to Meg.

"What's that the little miss is holding," thought Coco. "Smells like me, but it isn't really like me...too small...too weak and puny."

Meg lowered Duncan onto the patio.

"Strange creature this. Better act like I'm boss. Assert yourself Coco." Coco straightened her tail, tensed all her muscles, flattened her ears and raised the hair on her back. As she took the stance of a terrier about to attack, she noticed her reflection in the patio sliding door.

"Mm, I do look vicious and not such a bad figure for a five year old. Muscles are strong…Oh yes, this little thing," Coco's eyes shifted back to Duncan. "You look like a rat but smell like a dog. Hey, where are you going?"

Duncan looked at the towering Staffordshire Bull Terrier and backed cautiously under Mom's long skirt and between her sandals.

"This seems a safe place," thought little Duncan.

Meg giggled, "Oh Mom, Dad, look. Duncan is hiding between Mom's sandals and under her long skirt. I can't believe it. Because he can't see Coco, he thinks Coco can't see him."

"I'm scared. I want my Mom," whimpered Duncan. "I don't understand why my Mom isn't here. Just you big guys wait. My Mom always protects me. She's bigger than me and she'll bark and frighten you all away."

"All be calm and allow the dogs to get to know each other. Stand still, Honey," Dad said to Mom.

"Coco won't hurt me. She's such a gentle soul. I know she won't hurt the puppy."

Coco sniffed, "Hey, you. What are you doing under Mom's skirt?" Coco poked her nose at the puppy.

"This isn't my Mom. My Mom looks a bit like you but is shorter and longer," whimpered Duncan to Coco as Coco's wet nose sniffed at him.

"Oh! Now I know what's going on. You are a pup," Coco chuckled. "This Mom is our Mom now. We belong to these humans. *They* are our pack leaders. Unfortunately, young one, you are not going to see your real Mom ever again."

"No! No! No!" Duncan came out from his hiding place. "You're telling a lie. My Mom would never desert me! Go away you horrid beast!" Duncan barked a little bark at Coco.

Coco had never had her own pups. She looked at little Duncan and saw the fear in his little eyes. Coco saw the tears that Duncan was so bravely trying to control. She saw him trembling with anxiety. Because she had never had her own puppies, she so badly wanted to look after a puppy.

"Come here, little one," Coco licked Duncan around

9

his ears. "I'll look after you. I'm big and strong and my teeth are long and sharp. No-one will harm you with me around."

"Okay. You can look after me, because I'm scared, but only until my Mom gets here," Duncan licked Coco on the nose.

"Coco and Duncan have become friends," squeaked Meg happily as she jumped up and down and around the patio.

Chapter 3

Scratches

"Meeow! Ssk! Hiss! Go away you little mutt. This is my place on the carpet!"

Scratches, the fifteen-year-old cat, arrogantly and ever so gracefully took her place in the sun in the family room.

"Earf!" Duncan barked a squeaky bark at Scratches. "Who says it's your place? You're not the boss of me!"

Duncan lowered his front paws and raised his tail in the air taunting Scratches.

"Ssskka! Phist!"

Quicker than a chameleon's tongue lashing out at an insect, Scratches unleashed a spiky claw that slashed at Duncan's nose.

"Yelp! Ow! Ouch! You wicked thing! You hurt me! Ow! Aooh!" Duncan whined and backed hastily away from Scratches.

The family, hearing the commotion, rushed in from the dining room where they were having breakfast.

"What's the matter Dunky?" Meg anxiously cuddled Duncan. "Oh no! You've hurt your nose." Duncan whined. It wasn't that sore, but he was enjoying the attention.

"I think Scratches had to put him in his place. It's a good thing too, she must show the dogs that she is not afraid of them. When Duncan grows a bit bigger he will be able to hurt her," Mom explained and gave Scratches a smooth rub on her coat.

"Purrr! Purrr! I love to be loved," Scratches arched her back upwards against the massaging hand. The contented grin on her face and her smirking eyes infuriated Duncan.

"Waf! Earf! Woof!" Duncan's little bark was squeaky but he eventually got his bark right. "You're a horrid, spiteful furry ball." Duncan squirmed out of Meg's hold.

"I am a cat!" Scratches sat up regally, and elegantly wafted her tail around her well-formed paws.

She was proud of herself, and rightly so, for she was indeed a beautiful creature.

"No, Duncan! Bad boy!" Dad intervened, "don't bark at Scratches."

Duncan retreated into Meg's hands, where she was crouching on the carpet.

"Humph! What's going on here! What have I missed?" Coco burst into the family room like a tornado, causing the loose rug on the floor to crumple up at the sliding door. She had the wide happy grin she always wore when she had been dashing around outside. Her tongue sloshed and slopped out the corner of her mouth. "Hey! Scratch old girl, what did I miss?"

Scratches turned her head slowly, serenely and blinked two slow blinks at Coco.

"Coco, darling Coco, please stop slobbering all over me. This little twit of a mutt tried to take my place on the carpet in the sun."

Scratches then with absolute grace licked a paw. "Really, what is the world coming to when certain individuals don't know their place," she complained.

"Okay, let's finish breakfast," Mom turned towards the dining room. "The pets have made friends with each other. Our eggs are getting cold."

"Come along Meg. Duncan has Coco to watch over him," Dad gently patted Meg on the shoulder. The family continued with breakfast.

As the human conversation droned on in the

15

background, Scratches twirled her aching old bones into a ball. She breathed a deep sigh and smiled contentedly.

"Aah! This little family is growing. Ten years ago Meg was born. Five years ago, Coco came into our lives and now this little Duncan. Aah! Just a little storm in a little teacup. Best he knows his place though. Mmmpurrr! It's so warm in the sun! The sun helps these aging bones of mine. The carpet is so soft..." Scratches closed her weary eyes and slept.

The night before had been a long one for her, visiting the Tabby cat down the road. Delicious meal they'd had too. Tess, the Tabby, was owned by a family who enjoyed fish. Last night, Tess and Scratches found a whole mound of sardine bones, which were absolutely delectable to lick clean. Scratches licked her lips as she dreamed.

"Come on, little one, let me show you the garden. Lots to do in this garden." Coco nudged Duncan out through the glass sliding door back onto the patio and out onto the green grass.

Chapter 4

The Lizards

Coco sprinted down the sloping grassy embankment and turned when she reached the bottom. "C'mon Dunky!"

"It's too steep," whined Duncan. "I'm not sure of this grass; it's hard and pricks my paws. It's not like my old home! I want to go back home to my old home! I want my Mom!" Duncan sobbed.

Coco, tongue flapping loosely from her grinning mouth, trudged up the grassy slope, "Aah gee, Duncan, don't start crying again."

Coco gently licked Duncan's nose. "Look at what fun you can have on this grassy slope. Look at me! Look at me!"

Coco rolled over onto her back and twisted first left and then right. With this snake-like movement, she was able to move right down the grassy slope. Duncan stared at Coco in amazement. This seemed a whole lot of fun. He rolled over onto his back and wriggled and wormed his way down the slope.

"Yippee! This is fun!" Duncan reached the bottom and started once more up the slope.

Coco galloped heavily passed him. She wasn't as fit as she should have been but this was because she much preferred lying lazily in the sun, rather than cavorting around the garden. Tongue flapping wildly between her grinning teeth, she reached the top of the grassy slope before Duncan.

"Haaph! Aaph! This is great fun isn't it," panted Coco. Once more the two dogs wriggled and wiggled down the slope.

"Ooh, it feels so soothing on my back," Duncan closed his eyes in satisfaction and lay recovering from his last "wriggle" down the slope. He rolled over onto his tummy, eyes shut. He heard a rustle of leaves. His lazy eyelids slowly allowed his eyes to peep into the sunshine. But, it wasn't only sunshine and Coco that he saw. A long animal, smaller than

him, was also lying on its tummy nearby. It had four paws. It had a tail longer than its body. The tail was as thick as the body and then tapered to almost nothing.

Duncan, still on his tummy, slowly crawled closer to the strange animal. The animal lay completely still. Its eyes remained fixed. The eyes stared and stared. Duncan felt a little afraid. He backed up a little, and then crawled forward a little. The animal seemed to be alive. It seemed to be able to see, but somehow it was frozen. Duncan stretched out his long neck and sniffed at the small dwarf animal. In a flash the animal's mouth opened. It hissed. It turned quickly. It dashed up the garden fence. It disappeared through a crack at the top of the fence.

Startled, Duncan jumped onto all fours and barked a ferocious little bark.

Coco, tongue hanging gleefully out of her mouth, barked jokingly at Duncan, "Hey you crazy pup. What has got you mad this time?"

"Dddid yyou ssee ththat?" Duncan rushed to the fence. Placing his front paws up onto the wood, he tried to climb the fence.

This made Coco burst out laughing. "Sorry Dunk, no I didn't see it. What?" Coco tried hard not to make Duncan feel bad, but it was really very funny to see a little puppy trying to climb a fence to try and reach a crack. Again and again, he tried to reach the crack. Coco was overcome with laughter. The harder she tried not to laugh, the more difficult it became to stop laughing.

Duncan turned on her. "Stop it! I saw this animal. It was long and short and had a long tail and staring eyes. It was vicious and it roared at me."

21

"Roared at you!" Once again, Coco was overcome with laughter. "How could it roar at you? It must have been a lizard. It may have hissed at you but lizards don't roar!" Again Coco chuckled and chuckled, her tongue flapping at the side of her mouth.

Duncan dropped his front paws off the fence. His tail drooped between his legs. He hung his head in embarrassment. Everything was so strange in his new home. He turned his back on Coco and slowly walked away. He so badly wanted to go back to his Mom.

Coco bounded up to him, "I'm sorry but you looked so funny. You looked like a dog trying to be a cat. I'm sorry. I'm really sorry. Please forgive me. That little animal is a lizard. Yes, they do look scary. They scare me too sometimes, but they can't hurt you. There are

loads of them in this garden. Come on, I'll show you."

Duncan followed Coco and was amazed to see how many lizards lived in the garden.

Duncan spent the rest of the first day in his new home foraging for lizards. Coco didn't of course. She preferred to laze in the warm sun watching energetic little Duncan. But from that day on, Duncan had a personal vendetta against the lizards. He was out to get them. He was determined to catch one of them to prove to Coco that he was braver than the lizards. They had made Coco laugh at him and he was going to get back at them.

Chapter 5

A Frightening Experience

As the days passed, Duncan grew from being a shy, little puppy into an independent, cheeky and loveable Miniature Daschund. Although the human family adored Coco, they found Duncan so delightful to watch. So did Coco and so did Scratches.

"Yip, yip yippee!" Duncan would hop, skip and jump down the grassy slope and into the flowerbeds.

"Mommy, we should have called Duncan, 'Jumpy'," remarked Meg one day to Mom, "he jumps like a rabbit on the grass."

Mom laughed, "Indeed, Meg you are so right. 'Jumpy' definitely says it all about Duncan."

Coco grinned widely as she watched Duncan jump in between the shrubs, and then over and then under.

Meg was in the garden too, practicing her hockey. She noticed a tennis ball, which the neighbours must have hit into the garden. She tossed the ball into the air. "Coco, come here girl," called Meg. "Fetch!" Meg threw the tennis ball across the grass.

Coco glanced at the ball and then at Meg. She glanced back at the ball and again at Meg. "I have been lying in the sun all morning and now you expect me to chase that ball. No way!"

"Come on, Coco! Fetch the ball," coaxed Meg.

It was the summer holidays. It was hot. Dad had gone to work as usual and Mom was busy in her home-office. Meg enjoyed playing with her pets during the holidays, as she was always so busy during school term.

"Coco! Come on! Fetch the ball!" Meg's blue eyes smiled at Coco, as she gently pushed Coco in the direction of the ball.

"Umph! Ok, ok! I'll get it for you." Coco lumbered across the garden to fetch the ball.

She returned to Meg, at a slow trot, the ball clutched between her teeth. Meg tried to take the ball out of Coco's mouth. Coco tightened her jaw. Meg wanted to play so she was going to tease Meg.

Her grip was extremely tight. She was a Staffordshire Bull Terrier and proud of her bite. Meg pulled at the tennis ball. Coco's big brown eyes teased Meg. Meg's little fingers tried to open Coco's tight jaw. Meg tugged and tugged. Coco waited patiently and just as Meg took another hard tug, Coco released the ball. Meg fell backwards onto the grass. She quickly scrambled back onto her feet and chased a grinning Coco around the garden.

"You tricked me, you little mongrel," laughed Meg. "I'm not a mongrel," panted Coco her tongue flapping wildly, "I'm a pedigree."

Meg couldn't understand what Coco was panting about and again she cajoled Coco, "I'll catch you and throw you into the pool."

SPLASH!

"Help!" Duncan's little bark came from the pool.

Coco stopped galloping around the garden and lifted her ears to hear better.

"H..h..elp!" Duncan's gurgling bark came from the direction of the pool.

Meg had also stopped to listen. Another soft gurgle and splash came from the pool. Meg and Coco ran towards the pool. Meg saw Duncan sinking into the water at the deepest end

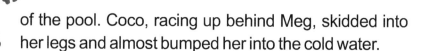

of the pool. Coco, racing up behind Meg, skidded into her legs and almost bumped her into the cold water.

"Mom!" shrieked Meg. "Mom! Please help!" Meg then dived into the pool.

From the home-office upstairs, Mom was able to look down onto the pool and garden. Every now and then, she would glance down to check if Meg was safe. She heard Meg screaming. Abruptly she ended the conversation she was having on the phone. What was happening to her little girl?

Her heartbeat echoed her racing feet as she sprinted down the stairs.

Meg felt the cold water hitting her sun burnt face as she dived into the pool.

No, oh no! Duncan could not die now. He was only two months old. Why, oh why had she not been watching him? She was angry with herself as she swam to the deeper water.

Duncan could not be seen on the surface of the pool. Holding her nose, so that water wouldn't enter her nostrils, Meg ducked her head under the water.

"There he is," thought Meg anxiously. She dived down to Duncan. Her frantic hands stretched out and grasped the little dog close to her chest. Her denim jeans were heavy around her legs. Her tackies, filled with water, made it difficult for her to tread water. She had to swim to the side of the pool! She had to do this to save herself and Duncan!

Duncan swallowed and swallowed. There was just too much water for a little dog to drink. What had happened to him? He remembered chasing the Indian Myna away from Scratches' food.

"You can't catch me. You can't fly up here. You can't even climb up here. You are a baby! You are a baby! You are a baby!"

The silly bird had teased him up in the tree above the pool. Duncan had tried to climb up the trunk of the tree. He had seen Scratches doing it and he was her size, so he thought he could climb as well as she. It was then that he lost his balance. He remembered falling into the pool.

A giant water bowl!

No matter how hard he tried to drink all the water, there was just too much water!

He tried to walk. He tried to run. But it was pointless. There wasn't any floor for his paws to reach. However, by moving his paws, he did discover that he was moving even though he wasn't touching the floor. He could swim!

He was able to reach the side of this enormous water bowl, but he was unable to lift himself out of the water. He tried again and again to lift himself, but the water kept dragging him under. He cried for help but no one heard him. As he became weaker and weaker from trying to lift himself out of the water, he kept swallowing water. His ears were blocked. All the water pushed his eyes closed. He was tired and the less he struggled, the more peaceful he felt. He slowly felt himself drifting into the calmness of the water. There was so much water. He felt part of the water. He drifted. Down, down, drifting peacefully, he relaxed.

All of a sudden, he felt himself being jerked upwards. He tried to open his eyes. Through the water, he saw a funny looking Meg. She was not clear. The water had made her look all smudged. Her blue eyes were enormous and her chestnut hair floated around her like twigs drifting around in his water bowl.

Duncan's thoughts faded to nothing.

Duncan felt the warmth of a fluffy towel around him. He felt Mom's comforting hands gently drying his ears. He felt water trickling from his nose. He tried to whine but as he opened his mouth, he coughed. Water, and more water, flowed from his mouth. Water! There was just so much water. He drifted into a hazy dream.

Through the haziness, he could see Meg. Water dripped down from her hair into her eyes.

Meg's tears mingled with the water.

"Dunky. Dunky. Oh, Dunky. I don't want you to die, Dunky."

Meg was cuddled up in a blanket. Her tears trickled down her cheeks.

Coco and Scratches sat either side of Meg. Both the animals stared with huge eyes at Duncan. As Duncan opened his eyes wider, Coco and Scratches shot over to where Mom was drying him. They realized Duncan would survive!

"He's okay. He is going to live. You saved Duncan, Meg!" Mom gave Meg a huge hug.

Meg leapt out of the blanket and grabbed Duncan in the fluffy towel and squeezed him close to her cheek.

The family room became the centre of a noisy celebration. Coco started barking and Scratches jumped up onto a couch to get a better view.

"I saved you, Dunky! You're alive."

Meg rocked Duncan backwards and forwards as she repeated the words over and over, tears of joy streaming down her face now.

"Hey little mutt, what a fright you gave us all today," grinned Coco, her tongue flapping out the side of her mouth.

"Little sweetheart, I…I could almost say I love you," purred Scratches. "Yes, I am sure of it, I do love you little darling. I would certainly have missed you dreadfully if you had drowned." Scratches twitched her tail. "But, enough with sentiment. I'm off to tell Tess, the Tabby cat, the whole exciting happening." Scratches scampered from the room. No, she couldn't be overcome with emotion. It would ruin her feline reputation for being indifferent.

Meg held Duncan cozily in her fluffy towel, while

she drank a cup of hot chocolate. When Mom placed a small bowl of hot chocolate down for Duncan, he struggled free of the towel and enjoyed lapping it up. The warm sensation seeped all through his body.

"You are a heroine, Meg," Mom praised Meg. "Dad will certainly be proud of your quick thinking that saved Duncan."

Duncan plodded wearily over to Meg. He licked her cold toes, no longer in the wet tackies.

Duncan then walked over to Coco, licked her under the chin and slowly walked over to the glass sliding door. He could see Scratches at the bottom of the garden. "I love you too, Scratchy!" he barked weakly.

Scratches turned her head haughtily and gave an affectionate "Meeoow".

Duncan grinned his naughty grin. He loved all of them, each and everyone of his new family. He loved his new home.

Duncan heard Dad's car pulling into the garage and darted to the front door so he could be the first to welcome Dad home. Meg, Mom and Coco followed.

What a frightening experience they had endured. Meg was eager to tell Dad about her heroic deed.

Duncan says you may not understand the meaning of all the words in his story. Here is a list of words, which Duncan did not understand:

Chapter 1

Miniature Daschund. The Standard Daschund had its beginnings in Germany where they joined their masters on hunting trips. The foresters and gamekeepers needed an active dog that would join them on hunting trips.

The dogs couldn't be too big as the hunters needed to keep up with the dogs and the dogs had to be fearless. The Miniature type was bred to hunt smaller animals like rabbits.

Staffordshire Bull Terrier was first bred in Great Britain. They were a combination of the Bulldog and the English Terrier. This combination made for a dog that was excellent at the sport of "pit fighting" which the miners and ironworkers of the time enjoyed. They were taught by their owners to fight and their instinct to do so was valued and respected. When dog fighting was outlawed, the dogs were seen to have other wonderful qualities such as intelligence, loyalty and devotion. They are now thought of as outstanding family dogs that protect their families.

Focused. Look clearly.

Blurred and **Blurring**. Unclear or hazy.

Introduce. To make a stranger known to another.

Beckoned. To make a sign to others by nodding or waving.

CHAPTER 2

Puny. Of small size and strength.

Stance. The position when preparing to do something.

Reflection. What you see when you look into a mirror.

Whimpered. Cried softly.

Chuckled. Quiet laugh to oneself.

Pack leaders. The ones who lead the group.

Anxiety. Uneasy. Nervous. Worried.

CHAPTER 3

Arrogantly. With pride. A bit bossy.

Taunting. Mock or make fun of.

Chameleon. A type of lizard that catches insects with its very quick tongue.

Commotion. Noise or upset.

Anxiously. Nervously or uneasily.

Attention. Fuss and care.

Contented. Happy.

Smirking. Smile as if you know more than someone else. Mocking smile.

Infuriated. Make very cross or angry.

Eventually. Finally.

Regally. Like a king or queen.

Elegantly. Graceful. With care.

Wafted. Float easily and gently.

Intervened. Interrupted or stopped.

Tornado. A whirlwind or as it is sometimes called, a twister, that takes place during a very bad storm.

Twit. Stupid person.

Mutt. A street dog. A mongrel.

Complained. To tell why you are unhappy or have problems.

Contentedly. Happily.

Storm in a tea cup. Nothing to be worried about.

Delectable. Very tasty. Delicious.

CHAPTER 4

Embankment. Mound of earth.

Trudged. Plod. To walk in a tired way.

Cavorting. To dance around or walk in a happy way.

Ferocious. Very fierce.

Overcome. To be overpowered or feel deeply about something.

Embarrassment. Shy, uneasy and feel silly.

Foraging. Searching or looking.

Preferred. To choose above anything else.

Energetic. Full of life. Very active.

Vendetta. To take revenge or settle a score.

Determined. To never give up.

CHAPTER 5

Coaxed. To encourage.

Lumbered. To walk heavily and lazily.

Trot. Not a walk nor a run.

Cajoled. To encourage by playing.

Galloping. Run fast.

Echoed. Make the same sound as.

Sprinted. Run fast and quickly.

Anxiously. Nervously. Worried.

Frantic. Wildly upset.

Tread. To kick in water in order to stay on top or afloat.

Indian Myna. A noisy bird that lives in cities and towns. It feeds on open lawns and fields and along roadsides. It is generally considered a pest or a nuisance.

Pointless. Of no use. Made no difference

Smudged. Not clear. Blurred.

Sentiment. Feeling or emotion